The *Unknown* SOLDIER

THE Unknown SOLDIER

Jess M. Brallier ★ Illustrated by Jamie Peterson

Charlesbridge

To my dad and my brother, JK, for their service and love—J. M. B.

To my three Ls and every freedom-loving American—J. P.

Published by Charlesbridge
9 Galen Street
Watertown, MA 02472
(617) 926-0329
www.charlesbridge.com

Printed in China
(hc) 10 9 8 7 6 5 4 3 2 1

Illustrations done in ink and watercolor on hot-pressed watercolor paper
Display type set in Uncle Edward by David Kerkhoff
Text type set in Beton by Adobe Systems Incorporated
Color separations by Boston Photo Imaging, Boston, MA
Printed by 1010 Printing International Limited in Huizhou, Guangdong, China
Production supervision by Jennifer Most Delaney
Designed by Diane M. Earley

Library of Congress Cataloging-in-Publication Data
Names: Brallier, Jess M., author. | Peterson, Jamie, illustrator.
Title: The unknown soldier / by Jess M. Brallier; illustrated by Jamie Peterson.
Description: Watertown, MA: Charlesbridge, [2022] | Includes bibliographical references. | Audience: Ages 5–9. | Audience: Grades 2–3. | Summary: "On a family trip to Washington, DC, Jack watches the soldier guarding the Tomb of the Unknowns and gains new understanding and respect for those who serve in the United States armed forces. Includes information about the Tomb and the soldiers who guard it."—Provided by publisher.
Identifiers: LCCN 2021029133 (print) | LCCN 2021029134 (ebook) | ISBN 9781623541590 (hardcover) | ISBN 9781632899439 (ebook)
Subjects: LCSH: Tomb of the Unknowns (Va.)—Juvenile fiction. | War memorials—Virginia—Juvenile fiction. | Honor guards—Juvenile fiction. | Soldiers—United States—Juvenile fiction. | Arlington (Va.)—Juvenile fiction. | Washington (D.C.)—Juvenile fiction. | CYAC: Tomb of the Unknowns (Va.)—Fiction. | Soldiers—Fiction. | Washington (D.C.)—Fiction. | LCGFT: Picture books.
Classification: LCC PZ7.B73358 Un 2022 (print) | LCC PZ7.B73358 (ebook) | DDC 813.54 [E]—dc23
LC record available at https://lccn.loc.gov/2021029133
LC ebook record available at https://lccn.loc.gov/2021029134

Jack and his parents hurry off the plane, pick up their suitcases, and rush through the airport. He and his mom high-five. "Vacation!"

Jack's dad points to a door behind a row of seats.

"Let's get out of here," says Jack's dad.

"What do you want to see first?" asks Jack's mom.

EXIT

Over the next two days, Jack visits large
memorials and important buildings.

He takes photos, eats hot dogs, and meets
somebody important from back home.

He pretends to be a spy, feeds zoo animals, and sees a real space capsule.

He enjoys a boat ride on a famous river.
The breeze is cooling, and the guide is funny.

On the last day of vacation, they visit
a large cemetery.
It's quiet and still.
Boring, thinks Jack.
But his parents insist.

They walk past rows of graves.
One after another.
Thousands of them.

They gather with others in another part
of the cemetery.

Jack watches. His mom told him to count.
A soldier marches twenty-one steps.
She stops, turns, her boots click, and she
pauses for twenty-one seconds.

Jack sips from his water bottle.
The sun is high and burning.
Not a cloud or breeze.

Jack wears shorts and a T-shirt.
The soldier wears a dark blue uniform.

The soldier turns, her boots click, and she pauses again for twenty-one seconds.

Jack counts. She marches twenty-one steps, back to where she started.

She guards the grave behind her, the
Tomb of the Unknown Soldier.
People watch in silence.
A few in uniform. Families. Couples.
Some older folks.

Caps held in hand.
Tears fall from the eyes of several.

Jack turns back to the guard.
Sweat drips from her face.
She ignores it.
Jack wipes his face again.

The guard is soon replaced by another soldier. Jack's mom explains that he'll be replaced in another half hour.

The soldiers guard the tomb. All day. Day after day. Month after month. Year after year.

Wow, Jack wonders, *who is this unknown soldier they're guarding?*

After lunch they visit other memorials.
At one place Jack's dad talks of his grandfather.

At another his mom touches the name
of an uncle she never knew.
Jack listens and watches.

That evening they return to the airport.
Vacation is over.

Jack looks out the taxi's window.
There's that cemetery again.
Jack closes his eyes and remembers.

Beyond the cemetery's closed gate, a lone soldier marches twenty-one steps.

She stops, turns, her boots click, and she pauses for twenty-one seconds.

Jack opens his eyes as the taxi arrives at
the airport.

Inside, the once-crowded terminal is now quiet.
A soldier naps at the end of the row of seats.

Jack remembers the words written on the tomb:
Here rests in honored glory an American soldier known but to God.

"Wait," says Jack to his mom.

He runs over to the soldier and whispers,
"Thank you, sir."

The man's eyes open. He smiles.

As Jack runs back to his parents, he hears, "Hey! Kid."
Jack turns around.

The unknown soldier now stands at full attention.
"You're welcome."

★ THE TOMB OF THE UNKNOWN SOLDIER ★

Arlington National Cemetery, Virginia

Wars are often confusing and violent. The bodies of fallen soldiers may be lost or impossible to identify. When this happens, the soldier's family can be told only that their loved one is missing. There will be no funeral—no chance to say goodbye and thank you. No grave for family and friends to visit.

To honor all unknown soldiers, the body of an American soldier killed in World War I was placed in a tomb at Arlington National Cemetery near Washington, DC, in November 1921. Since midnight on July 2, 1937, when a special guard unit was formed, there has been a twenty-four-hour watch over the tomb, regardless of weather conditions or world events.

In front of the tomb, a guard marches twenty-one steps, stops and turns to face the tomb for twenty-one seconds, turns to face the other direction, shifts the rifle to their outer shoulder, pauses for twenty-one seconds, then repeats the process.

The guard carries the rifle on the shoulder closest to visitors as a gesture of protecting the tomb against any threat. The number twenty-one represents the twenty-one gun salute, the highest of military honors. The timing of the changing of the guard depends on the season and time of day. New and old guards switch places after the tomb is saluted and the weapon of the new guard is inspected.

Only twenty percent of the soldiers who volunteer to guard the Tomb of the Unknown Soldier are even considered. They must have a perfect military record, be highly motivated and disciplined, and possess a strong military bearing and soldierly appearance. They start their long days at 5:00 a.m. and are regularly reviewed and tested. Their uniforms are closely inspected, even down to the distances between the medals worn on their jackets. These medals include one with a likeness of the tomb, inscribed with the words *Honor Guard*. Because of the exhausting intensity of their duty, few guards serve for more than two years. As one guard has said, "You have to be perfect."*

At the Tomb of the Unknown Soldier, soldiers who made the ultimate sacrifice are honored. Thankful citizens can express their appreciation. Families and friends can say farewell and "I love you forever." A visit to the tomb, to thoughtfully watch and listen, can create memories for a lifetime, as it does for Jack in this story.

*Quoted in Roger Wachtel, *The Tomb of the Unknown Soldier* (New York: Children's Press, 2003), 36.